This Little Tiger book belongs to:

_____

_____

_____

zzzzzZZZZZZZZZZZZZZZzzzzzzzzzzzz

PRESS THE PAGE

HEAR THE NOISE!

For Andrea & Claudia
— I F

For Mum & Dad, who helped
— J T

LITTLE TIGER PRESS
An imprint of Magi Publications
1 The Coda Centre, 189 Munster Road, London SW6 6AW
www.littletigerpress.com

First published in Great Britain 1999
This edition published 2011
Text copyright © Isobel Finn 1999
Illustrations copyright © Jack Tickle 1999
Isobel Finn and Jack Tickle have asserted their rights
to be identified as the author and illustrator of this work
under the Copyright, Designs and Patents Act, 1988
A CIP catalogue record for this book is available
from the British Library

ISBN 978-1-84895-220-1
LTP/1800/0309/0811
Printed in China
2 4 6 8 10 9 7 5 3

The Very Lazy Ladybird

Isobel Finn & Jack Tickle

LITTLE TIGER PRESS
London

This is the story of
a very lazy ladybird.
She liked to sleep all day
and all night.

zzZZZZZZ

And because she slept
all day and all night,
this lazy ladybird didn't
know how to fly.

ZZZZZZZZZZZZZZZZZZZZzzzzzzz

One day the lazy ladybird
wanted to sleep
somewhere else.
But what could she do
if she couldn't fly?

Then the lazy ladybird
had a very good idea.
When a kangaroo bounded by . . .

she hopped into her pouch.

But the kangaroo liked to
JUMP!

"I can't sleep in here,"
cried the lazy ladybird.
"It's far too bumpy."

So when a tiger padded by . . .

she hopped on to his back.

But the tiger liked to

ROAR!

"I can't sleep here,"
said the lazy ladybird.
"It's far too noisy."

So when a crocodile swam by . . .

she hopped on to his tail.

S
S

But the crocodile liked to
swish his tail in the water.

WISH!

WISH!

"I can't sleep here,"
said the lazy ladybird.
"I'll fall into the river!"
So when a monkey
swung by . . .

she hopped on
to her head.

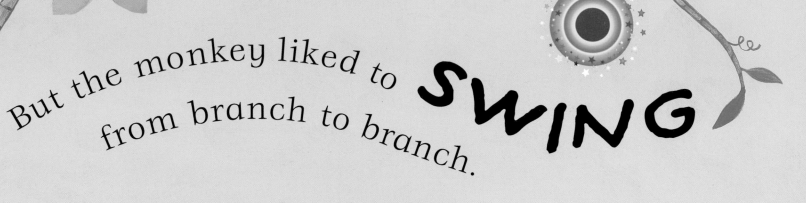

But the monkey liked to **SWING**
from branch to branch.

"I can't sleep here,"
said the lazy ladybird.
"I'm feeling dizzy."
So when a bear ambled by . . .

she hopped on to his ear.

But the bear
liked to

SCRATCH

SCR

ATCH

SCRATCH.

"I can't sleep here,"
said the lazy ladybird.
"He'll never sit still."
So when an elephant trundled by . . .

she hopped on
to his trunk.

"At last!" said the lazy ladybird.
"I've found someone
who doesn't . . .

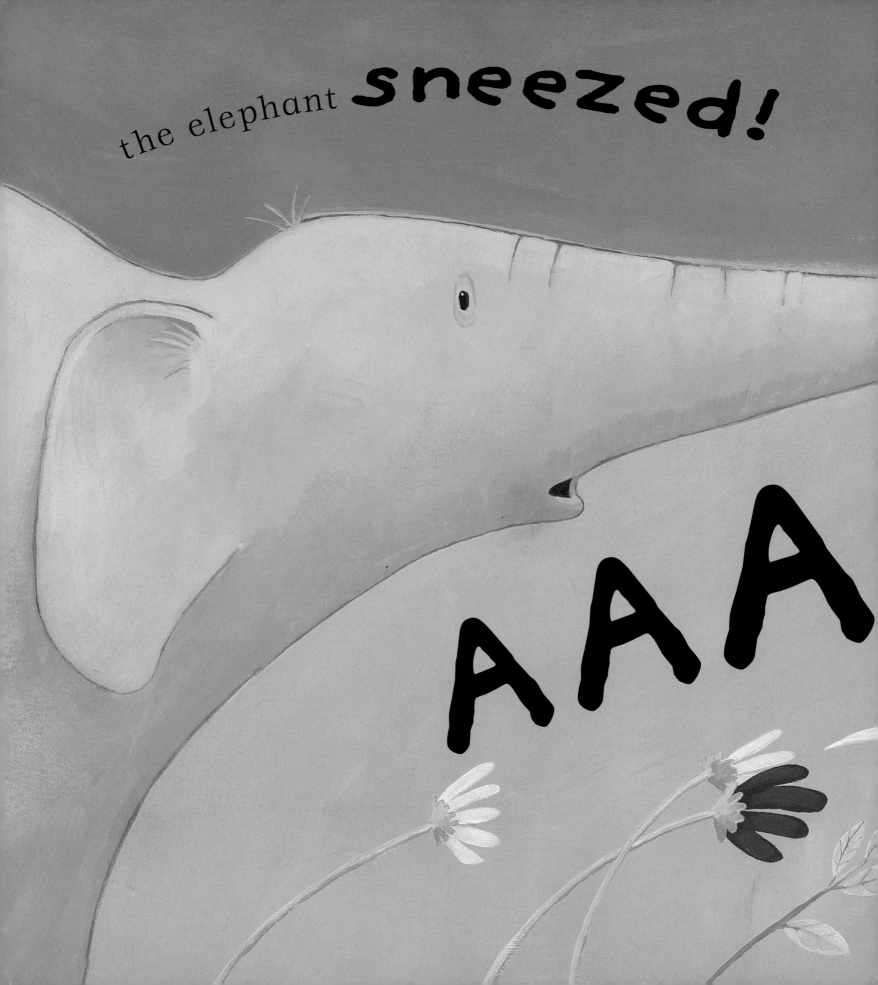

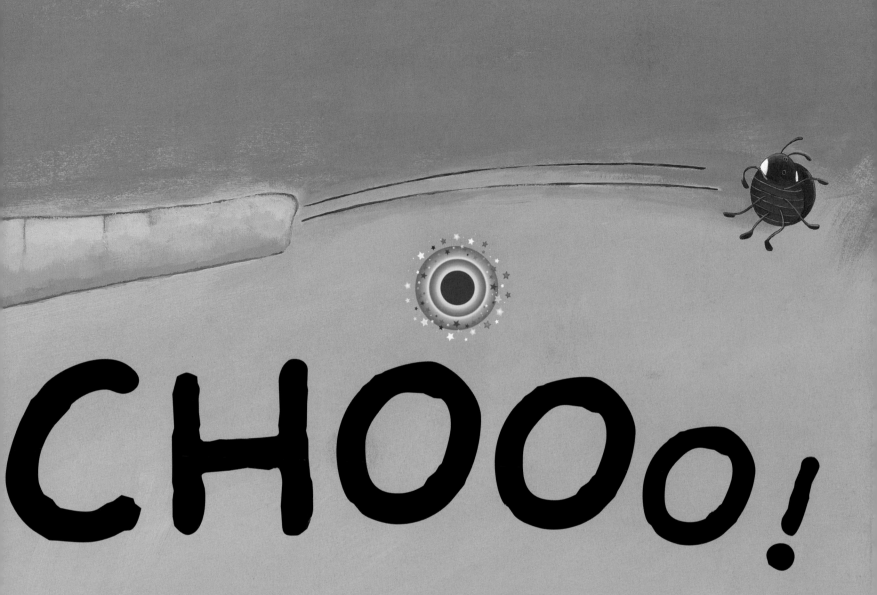

CHOOo!

and poor old lazy ladybird . . .

. . . had to fly
at last!

Aaaaaaaaahhh

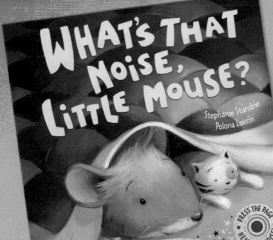